JANUARY 2026

Sunday	Monday	Tuesday	Wednesday	Thursday	Friday	Saturday
				1 New Year's Day	2	3
4	5	6	7	8	9	10
11	12	13	14	15	16	17
18	19 Martin Luther King, Jr. Day	20	21	22	23	24
25	26	27	28	29	30	31

NOTES

"I dreamed that you were all in white from head to heel, with a long pale cloak flowing from those broad shoulders. You were a White Sword, ser, a Sworn Brother of the Kingsguard."

FEBRUARY

GEORGE R. R. MARTIN

A KNIGHT OF THE SEVEN KINGDOMS

2026 CALENDAR ♦ ILLUSTRATIONS BY TOM KIDD

FEBRUARY 2026

Sunday	Monday	Tuesday	Wednesday	Thursday	Friday	Saturday
1	2 Groundhog Day	3	4	5	6	7
8	9	10	11	12	13	14 Valentine's Day
15	16 Presidents' Day	17 Ramadan begins	18	19	20	21
22	23	24	25	26	27	28

NOTES

Dunk had no notion where Lord Butterwell's bedchamber was to be found, but the other men pushed and prodded him until he got there.

MARCH

MARCH 2026

Sunday	Monday	Tuesday	Wednesday	Thursday	Friday	Saturday
1	2	3	4	5	6	7
8	9	10	11	12	13	14
15	16	17 St. Patrick's Day	18	19	20 Spring begins	21
22	23	24	25	26	27	28
29 Palm Sunday	30	31				

NOTES

Black Tom showed his teeth in a hard grin.
"I saw him try to joust."
"I am better with a sword," Dunk warned him.

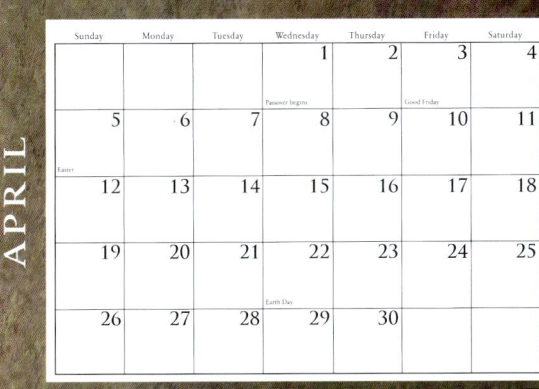

APRIL 2026

Sunday	Monday	Tuesday	Wednesday	Thursday	Friday	Saturday
			1 Passover begins	2	3 Good Friday	4
5 Easter	6	7	8	9	10	11
12	13	14	15	16	17	18
19	20	21	22 Earth Day	23	24	25
26	27	28	29	30		

NOTES

Mad Danelle Lothston herself rode forth in strength from her haunted towers at Harrenhal, clad in black armor that fit her like an iron glove, her long red hair streaming.

MAY

MAY 2026

Sunday	Monday	Tuesday	Wednesday	Thursday	Friday	Saturday
					1	2
3	4	5 Cinco de Mayo	6	7	8	9
10 Mother's Day	11	12	13	14	15	16
17	18	19	20	21	22	23
24	25	26	27	28	29	30
31 Memorial Day						

NOTES

A troupe of painted dwarfs came bursting from the belly of a wheeled wooden pig to chase Lord Butterwell's fool about the tables.

JUNE 2026

Sunday	Monday	Tuesday	Wednesday	Thursday	Friday	Saturday
	1	2	3	4	5	6
7	8	9	10	11	12	13
14 Flag Day	15	16	17	18	19 Juneteenth	20
21 Father's Day / Summer begins	22	23	24	25	26	27
28	29	30				

NOTES

"Someday the dragons will return. My brother Daeron's dreamed of it, and King Aerys read it in a prophecy. Maybe it will be my egg that hatches. That would be splendid."

JULY 2026

Sunday	Monday	Tuesday	Wednesday	Thursday	Friday	Saturday
			1	2	3	4 **Independence Day**
5	6	7	8	9	10	11
12	13	14	15	16	17	18
19	20	21	22	23	24	25
26	27	28	29	30	31	

NOTES

"The pie is meant to be the marriage, and a true marriage has in it many sorts of things—joy and grief, pain and pleasure, love and lust and loyalty. So it is fitting that there be birds of many sorts."

AUGUST

AUGUST 2026

Sunday	Monday	Tuesday	Wednesday	Thursday	Friday	Saturday
						1
2	3	4	5	6	7	8
9	10	11	12	13	14	15
16	17	18	19	20	21	22
23	24	25	26	27	28	29
30	31					

NOTES

Whitewalls was almost new as castles went, having been raised a mere forty years ago by the grandsire of its present lord.

SEPTEMBER

SEPTEMBER 2026

Sunday	Monday	Tuesday	Wednesday	Thursday	Friday	Saturday
		1	2	3	4	5
6	7 Labor Day	8	9	10	11 Rosh Hashanah	12
13	14	15	16	17	18	19
20 Yom Kippur / George R. R. Martin's Birthday	21	22 Autumn begins	23	24	25	26
27	28	29	30			

NOTES

Uthor's iron fist took him square between his eyes, with all the force of man and horse behind it.

OCTOBER 2026

Sunday	Monday	Tuesday	Wednesday	Thursday	Friday	Saturday
				1	2	3
4	5	6	7	8	9	10
11	12 *Indigenous Peoples' Day / Columbus Day*	13	14	15	16	17
18	19	20	21	22	23	24
25	26	27	28	29	30	31 *Halloween*

NOTES

"You can go into the water as you are, or you can go in bleeding. Which will it be?"

NOVEMBER 2026

Sunday	Monday	Tuesday	Wednesday	Thursday	Friday	Saturday
1	2	3	4	5	6	7
8	9	10	11 Veterans Day	12	13	14
15	16	17	18	19	20	21
22	23	24	25	26 Thanksgiving Day	27	28
29	30					

NOTES

"I dreamed of you and a dead dragon . . . A great beast, huge, with wings so large they could cover this meadow. It had fallen on top of you, but you were alive and the dragon was dead."

DECEMBER 2026

Sunday	Monday	Tuesday	Wednesday	Thursday	Friday	Saturday
		1	2	3	4	5
					Hanukkah begins	
6	7 Pearl Harbor Remembrance Day	8	9	10	11	12
13	14	15	16	17	18	19
20 Winter begins	21	22	23	24	25 Christmas Day	26 Kwanzaa begins
27	28	29	30	31 New Year's Eve		

They had heard such talk before, in winesinks and low taverns, and around campfires in the woods.

JANUARY 2027

FEBRUARY 2027

$18.00 U.S. $24.95 CAN

ISBN 978-0-593-87330-4

No part of this calendar may be used or reproduced in any manner for the purpose of training artificial intelligence technologies or systems.

EU Contact: Penguin Random House Ireland, 32 Nassau Street, Dublin D02 YH68, https://eu-contact.penguin.ie

Published in the United States by Random House Worlds, an imprint of Random House, a division of Penguin Random House LLC, New York, 1745 Broadway, New York, NY 10019, prh.com

Printed in China on acid-free paper by C&C Offset.

Calendar and illustrations © 2025 by WO & Shade LLC. All rights reserved.

georgerrmartin.com
Facebook.com/georgerrmartinofficial · X: @GRRMspeaking
tomkidd.myportfolio.com

JANUARY 2026

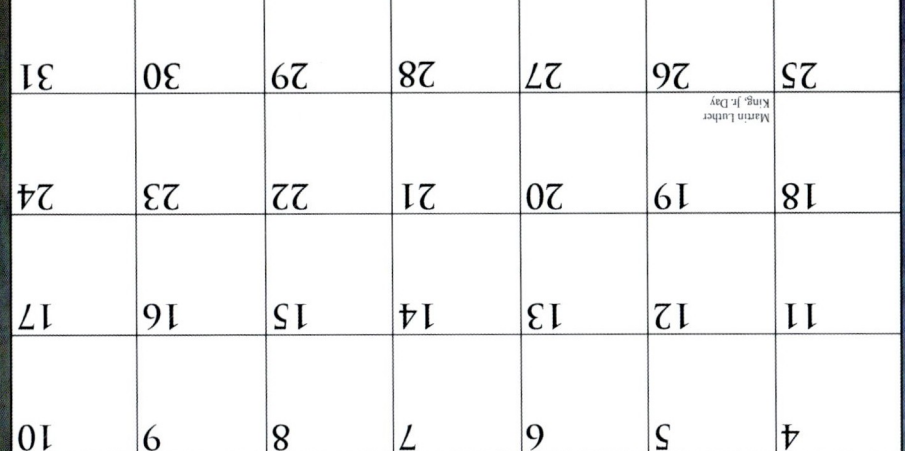

FEBRUARY

"I dreamed that you were all in white from head to heel, with a long, pale cloak flowing from those broad shoulders. You were a White Sword, ser, a Sworn Brother of the Kingsguard."

NOTES

Sunday	Monday	Tuesday	Wednesday	Thursday	Friday	Saturday
				1	2	3
4	5	6	7 New Year's Day	8	9	10
11	12	13	14	15	16	17
18	19 Martin Luther King, Jr. Day	20	21	22	23	24
25	26	27	28	29	30	31

13 stunning illustrations—including a bonus fold-out poster!

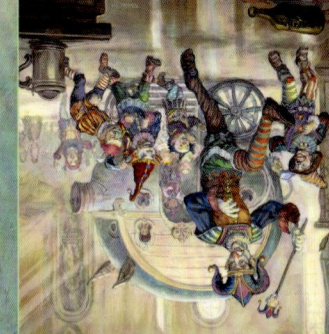

Artist Tom Kidd takes us to the time of a lowly hedge knight known as Dunk and his trusty squire, Egg, for this calendar inspired exclusively by George R. R. Martin's collection of Westeros novellas, *A Knight of the Seven Kingdoms*.

In the same year as HBO's release of *A Knight of the Seven Kingdoms*, this collection of twelve all-new images, plus one bonus poster, offers a fresh glimpse into the world of Dunk and Egg—one filled with tourneys and feasts, weddings and widows, as the naïve hedge knight and his young squire travel the land, becoming caught up in plots and treason and bids for power.

JANUARY 2026

Sunday	Monday	Tuesday	Wednesday	Thursday	Friday	Saturday
				1 New Year's Day	2	3
4	5	6	7	8	9	10
11	12	13	14	15	16	17
18	19 Martin Luther King, Jr. Day	20	21	22	23	24
25	26	27	28	29	30	31

NOTES

"I dreamed that you were all in white from head to heel, with a long pale cloak flowing from those broad shoulders. You were a White Sword, ser, a Sworn Brother of the Kingsguard."

GEORGE R. R. MARTIN

A Knight of the Seven Kingdoms

2026 CALENDAR • ILLUSTRATIONS BY TOM KIDD

FEBRUARY 2026

Sunday	Monday	Tuesday	Wednesday	Thursday	Friday	Saturday
1	2 Groundhog Day	3	4	5	6	7
8	9	10	11	12	13	14 Valentine's Day
15	16 Presidents' Day	17 Ramadan begins	18	19	20	21
22	23	24	25	26	27	28

NOTES

Dunk had no notion where Lord Butterwell's bedchamber was to be found, but the other men pushed and prodded him until he got there.

MARCH

MARCH 2026

Sunday	Monday	Tuesday	Wednesday	Thursday	Friday	Saturday
1	2	3	4	5	6	7
8	9	10	11	12	13	14
15	16	17 St. Patrick's Day	18	19	20 Spring begins	21
22	23	24	25	26	27	28
29 Palm Sunday	30	31				

NOTES

Black Tom showed his teeth in a hard grin.
"I saw him try to joust."
"I am better with a sword," Dunk warned him.

APRIL 2026

Sunday	Monday	Tuesday	Wednesday	Thursday	Friday	Saturday
			1 Passover begins	2	3 Good Friday	4
5 Easter	6	7	8	9	10	11
12	13	14	15	16	17	18
19	20	21	22 Earth Day	23	24	25
26	27	28	29	30		

NOTES

Mad Danelle Lothston herself rode forth in strength from her haunted towers at Harrenhal, clad in black armor that fit her like an iron glove, her long red hair streaming.

MAY 2026

Sunday	Monday	Tuesday	Wednesday	Thursday	Friday	Saturday
					1	2
3	4	5 *Cinco de Mayo*	6	7	8	9
10 *Mother's Day*	11	12	13	14	15	16
17	18	19	20	21	22	23
24 / 31 *Memorial Day*	25	26	27	28	29	30

NOTES

A troupe of painted dwarfs came bursting from the belly of a wheeled wooden pig to chase Lord Butterwell's fool about the tables.

JUNE

JUNE 2026

Sunday	Monday	Tuesday	Wednesday	Thursday	Friday	Saturday
	1	2	3	4	5	6
7	8	9	10	11	12	13
14 **Flag Day**	15	16	17	18	19 **Juneteenth**	20
21 **Father's Day / Summer begins**	22	23	24	25	26	27
28	29	30				

NOTES

"Someday the dragons will return. My brother Daeron's dreamed of it, and King Aerys read it in a prophecy. Maybe it will be my egg that hatches. That would be splendid."

JULY 2026

Sunday	Monday	Tuesday	Wednesday	Thursday	Friday	Saturday
			1	2	3	4 Independence Day
5	6	7	8	9	10	11
12	13	14	15	16	17	18
19	20	21	22	23	24	25
26	27	28	29	30	31	

NOTES

"The pie is meant to be the marriage, and a true marriage has in it many sorts of things—joy and grief, pain and pleasure, love and lust and loyalty. So it is fitting that there be birds of many sorts."

AUGUST 2026

Sunday	Monday	Tuesday	Wednesday	Thursday	Friday	Saturday
						1
2	3	4	5	6	7	8
9	10	11	12	13	14	15
16	17	18	19	20	21	22
23	24	25	26	27	28	29
30	31					

NOTES

Whitewalls was almost new as castles went, having been raised a mere forty years ago by the grandsire of its present lord.

SEPTEMBER

SEPTEMBER 2026

Sunday	Monday	Tuesday	Wednesday	Thursday	Friday	Saturday
		1	2	3	4	5
6	7 *Labor Day*	8	9	10	11 *Rosh Hashanah*	12
13	14	15	16	17	18	19
20 *Yom Kippur / George R. R. Martin's Birthday*	21	22 *Autumn begins*	23	24	25	26
27	28	29	30			

NOTES

Uthor's iron fist took him square between his eyes, with all the force of man and horse behind it.

OCTOBER

OCTOBER 2026

Sunday	Monday	Tuesday	Wednesday	Thursday	Friday	Saturday
				1	2	3
4	5	6	7	8	9	10
11	12 Indigenous Peoples' Day / Columbus Day	13	14	15	16	17
18	19	20	21	22	23	24
25	26	27	28	29	30	31 Halloween

NOTES

"You can go into the water as you are, or you can go in bleeding. Which will it be?"

NOVEMBER 2026

Sunday	Monday	Tuesday	Wednesday	Thursday	Friday	Saturday
1	2	3	4	5	6	7
8	9	10	11 Veterans Day	12	13	14
15	16	17	18	19	20	21
22	23	24	25	26 Thanksgiving Day	27	28
29	30					

NOTES

"I dreamed of you and a dead dragon . . . A great beast, huge, with wings so large they could cover this meadow. It had fallen on top of you, but you were alive and the dragon was dead."

DECEMBER 2026

Sunday	Monday	Tuesday	Wednesday	Thursday	Friday	Saturday
		1	2	3	4 Hanukkah begins	5
6	7 Pearl Harbor Remembrance Day	8	9	10	11	12
13	14	15	16	17	18	19
20 Winter begins	21	22	23	24	25 Christmas Day	26 Kwanzaa begins
27	28	29	30	31 New Year's Eve		

They had heard such talk before, in winesinks and low taverns, and around campfires in the woods.

JANUARY 2026

Sunday	Monday	Tuesday	Wednesday	Thursday	Friday	Saturday
				1 New Year's Day	2	3
4	5	6	7	8	9	10
11	12	13	14	15	16	17
18	19 Martin Luther King, Jr. Day	20	21	22	23	24
25	26	27	28	29	30	31

NOTES

"I dreamed that you were all in white from head to heel, with a long pale cloak flowing from those broad shoulders. You were a White Sword, ser, a Sworn Brother of the Kingsguard."

FEBRUARY

Artist Tom Kidd takes us to the time of a lowly hedge knight known as Dunk and his trusty squire, Egg, for this calendar inspired exclusively by George R. R. Martin's collection of Westeros novellas, *A Knight of the Seven Kingdoms*.

In the same year as HBO's release of *A Knight of the Seven Kingdoms*, this collection of twelve all-new images, plus one bonus poster, offers a fresh glimpse into the world of Dunk and Egg—one filled with tourneys and feasts, weddings and widows, as the naïve hedge knight and his young squire travel the land, becoming caught up in plots and treason and bids for power.

 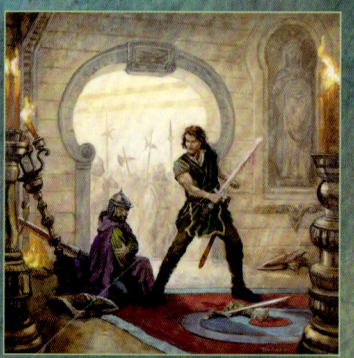 

13 stunning illustrations—including a bonus fold-out poster!

Calendar and illustrations © 2025 by WO & Shade LLC. All rights reserved.
georgerrmartin.com   Facebook.com/georgerrmartinofficial   X: @GRRMspeaking
tomkidd.myportfolio.com

$18.00 U.S. $24.95 CAN
ISBN 978-0-593-87330-4

Published in the United States by Random House Worlds, an imprint of Random House, a division of Penguin Random House LLC, New York, 1745 Broadway, New York, NY 10019. prh.com
Printed in China on acid-free paper by C&C Offset.
EU Contact: Penguin Random House Ireland, 32 Nassau Street, Dublin D02 YH68. https://eu-contact.penguin.ie

No part of this calendar may be used or reproduced in any manner for the purpose of training artificial intelligence technologies or systems.